TIED UP BY THE BOSS

A FIRST TIME LESBIAN SPANKING

JOSIE BALE

TIED UP BY THE BOSS

© 2023 by Josie Bale

Cover by Reba Bale

CONTENTS

About This Book

She's inexperienced in the ways of the world, but not for long!

Marci has heard the rumors – senior staffers at her work are punishing their subordinates with **good hard spankings**. But it can't really be true, can it?

When the shy computer coder gets assigned to her secret crush for a high priority project, her anxiety gets in the way of her work performance, and she starts making big mistakes. Her boss Colleen offers her a choice: lose her job or allow the sexy older woman free reign to **break her** of her anxious thoughts.

Desperate to keep her position in the company, Marci finds herself **tied up** and experiencing the sting of a **firm**

paddling. To her surprise, the punishments settle her mind.

They also awaken a strong desire to have her first lesbian experience...but will her domme boss give her what she really needs?

"Tied Up By the Boss" is part of the Sapphic Submission series. These sexy and fun stories follow the adventures of the employees at WLW Technology, where getting in trouble can lead to bare bottomed punishments from the lesbians in charge. These books are intended for mature audiences.

Be sure to check out a free preview of book one of the Spanking Therapy Clinic series, "The Reluctant Bride's First Spanking" at the end of this book!

STAY IN TOUCH WITH JOSIE BALE

You can stay up to date on all of Josie Bale's sexy spanking stories by following her at https://www. amazon.com/author/josiebale. You'll receive an email notifying you of all new releases!

CHAPTER ONE: THE RUMORS ARE TRUE

"**Y**ou're telling me it's true? Everything?"

I leaned forward, my elbows resting on the table as I studied my new friends. Alina and Brandy nodded in unison, while Suzanne just shrugged.

"You're telling me that some of our employees are receiving spankings from the bosses?" I confirmed.

This time all three of them nodded.

"None of the bosses have ever laid a hand on me," Suzanne said. "But I've heard things coming from the offices that I can't really explain any other way."

She shivered.

"It sounds painful. And fun."

The smiles on Alina's and Brandy's faces told me that they could confirm Suzanne's assumptions.

"I can't go into detail," Alina said. "But I'll just say that sometimes I mess things up on purpose now, just so I can get some...personalized attention from my boss."

Everyone at the table laughed.

I'd been working at WLW Technology for a couple of months now and had heard rumors that the senior partners had an unusual way of correcting their employee's behavior: spanking.

I'd chalked it up to gossip until my office mate had wandered in this morning looking both sore and well satisfied. At first I'd thought she'd just gotten lucky last night, but then she yelped in pain as she sat down on her office chair, grumbling under her breath about how the belt wasn't necessary.

Too shocked and embarrassed to ask about it – I mean, what if I'd heard her wrong? – I decided to ask my lunchmates. These girls seemed to have very few inhibitions, so I felt totally comfortable asking them anything.

"How...how does it happen?"

Spanking employees? How could that possibly be allowed? I couldn't decide whether I was asking because I wanted to avoid it or encourage it. The slight dampening in my panties said it was the latter. I didn't want to examine my reaction too closely.

"I messed something up, big time," Alina said. "So Ruth gave me a hard spanking. It hurt like hell, but then it turned into...something more."

"They just moved in together," Suzanne whispered.

Alina nodded. "Yeah, and it's going great. She's even brought me to the secret BDSM club they all belong to."

"What about you, Brandy?" I asked.

"Sasha caught me eavesdropping on Alina and Ruth, so she decided to punish me. Then I showed her my appreciation, if you know what I mean."

I felt my cheeks turn a little pink at the innuendo. My entire life I'd fantasized about being with a woman. I'd masturbated to the idea of a stern older woman taking me under her control. But I'd never had a clue how to act on it.

The truth was I was shy. Painfully shy. That's why at twenty-four I was a virgin. I hadn't been with anyone – male or female – my entire life.

For years I'd been able to satisfy myself with the help of a battery operated boyfriend, but ever since I'd started working at WLW Technology I'd been obsessed with having sex with a woman. Obsessed. Probably because all the bosses were lesbians. Hot, sexy, stern lesbians – every single one of them.

Whenever I imagined having sex, I imagined a firm hand coming down hard on my bare ass. The bite of pain before the pleasure.

And I knew who I wanted to take my virginity: Colleen O'Keefe.

She was older than me by at least fifteen years. She was average height, maybe five six, with a slim figure other than breasts that were a little too big for her frame.

She looked as Irish as her name, with a long mane of curly red hair and green eyes. Her skin was pale as cream but covered with red freckles. I found myself spending hours in meetings fantasizing about whether those freckles were everywhere.

I'd never in a million years guess that Colleen was a domme. She had the sweetest face, always with a ready smile for people. But I'd heard rumors that she hung out at the BDSM club with the other bosses, and there wasn't a submissive among them. Clearly there was another side to her.

Colleen wasn't my direct supervisor, but she was a senior partner who was way higher on the food chain than I was. We worked on the same floor, and she supervised the other team who was collocated with mine. I couldn't imagine in what scenario I'd get closer to Colleen. But as luck would have it, an opportunity arose the very next day.

"Marci!"

I looked up to see my team lead standing by my desk. I'd been so lost in my coding work I hadn't heard her come up.

"Gail. What do you need?"

"Colleen needs another programmer to help her with a special assignment. I told her she could borrow you since you're just finishing up a project. You're being reassigned to her team until further notice."

"Really?"

Gail's eyes narrowed at my excitement. "Yeah, why?"

"Oh, well, I've been wanting to work with her."

"Whatever. She wants you to report to her office at one o'clock sharp for a briefing."

"Okay."

I presented myself to Colleen's office promptly at one o'clock. The door was open, so I rapped on the door jamb to announce my presence. Colleen looked up from her work, shrewd green eyes taking in my leggings and skater girl dress. The outfit made my legs look a mile long, and the dress flattered my waist and chest without making me look slutty. I loved it.

"Come on in, Marci," Colleen invited.

I walked into the space, sitting down on a chair across from her. Her office was large and bright, with a separate conference area on one side.

"Did you look at the specs I emailed you earlier today?" she asked.

"Yes ma'am."

Her green eyes darkened at the honorific.

"Good. You understand that this project is going to require long hours and probably some late nights over the next three weeks in order for us to meet the deadline?"

"Yes ma'am."

Colleen studied me carefully.

"This is an important project for the company, and it could lead to a huge contract for us," she explained. "If you do well, you will get a reward. If you fuck anything up, we're going to have a problem. Do you understand?"

"Yes ma'am."

"Good girl." Her eyes widened slightly as if she hadn't meant to say that. "I mean, great. We'll get started right away."

Chapter Two: Late Night Anxiety

I'd been working alongside Colleen on this project for two weeks now and it was all-consuming. Everyone on the team had been putting in crazy hours.

The coding was complicated, and the client was difficult, making a lot of last minute changes. Honestly, the pressure was getting to me. I was terrified of messing something up and letting down the team. Disappointing Colleen.

That's how I found myself on the verge of a panic attack late one night.

I'd made a small error. Nothing big, really. But it had messed something up in the code. Then I'd been so freaked out trying to fix it that I'd made it worse, and now I couldn't seem to figure out how to make it work. I was sitting at my desk with my head between my legs trying to breathe when I heard Colleen's voice. It was distorted, as if she were underwater.

"Marci! What's wrong."

"N—nothing," I gasped. It was hard to get in air with the extreme pressure on my chest.

I felt Colleen's hand stroke my blonde hair, petting me like a cat.

"Focus on something you can hear, like the sound of my voice," she instructed, her voice firmer than I'd ever heard it.

I complied, listening as she gently told me that I was going to be okay, that she was here for me.

"Now focus on something you can feel, like the sensation of my fingers on your scalp." She spread her fingers on the top of my head, slipping through the fine strands of my blonde hair, to massage my scalp.

My heart rate started to slow as my breathing evened out.

"Good girl. Now focus on something you smell."

I inhaled sharply, and my nose filled with the scent of Colleen's perfume. Or maybe it was her shampoo. Whatever it was, it smelled almost mossy, like the forest after a rain.

Slowly I lifted my head as air returned to my lungs and my heart resumed a more normal rate.

"I'm sorry," I whispered. "This has never happened before. At least not this bad."

"What triggered your anxiety attack?"

"I messed up the code," I said miserably. "Then I tried to fix it and I made it worse. Now I'm totally stuck, and I can't make it work."

Colleen studied my face for a long moment. "Come to my office please."

I pushed to my feet and trailed behind her, my eyes on the soft curve of her ass. Colleen was wearing high waisted pants and a snug fitting blouse that made her look like an Irish pin-up girl.

When we got to her office, Colleen closed the door behind us, the click of the lock sounding loud in the quiet space. My breathing became shallow again.

"You have good skills Marci," Colleen began. "I think you could go far here at WLW Technology, but what I'm seeing is that your intense anxiety gets in the way of your success. This project has really highlighted that for me."

She was right.

"I can't have less than one hundred percent from anyone on my team right now. I think I either need to find someone else for this project, or you need to find a way to shut off you mind, to focus on one thing without letting the anxious thoughts take over."

She walked around me until we were facing each other. When she spoke again, her voice was firmer than I'd ever heard it.

"I can help you if you want to keep your job, I know just what to do. But I must warn you that my methods are...unconventional. Do you want me to break you of your anxiety? Or do you want to find another job?"

I flashed back to the day at the cafeteria where I'd talked to my friends about the partners all being into BDSM. Was she implying what I thought she was?

"Answer me, young lady!"

The firm authority in Colleen's order simultaneously sent a rush of arousal to my core and calmed my racing mind.

"Yes."

"Yes, what?" She raised one red eyebrow.

"Yes, ma'am. I want you to...break me."

Her mouth quirked. "Very well. We will start now. Remove all your clothes."

"Umm..."

Colleen closed the distance between us, her fingers wrapping around my chin to force me to meet her gaze. Her eyes were cold.

"Did you not understand my instructions? Either you want my help, or you don't. If you don't, I'll need to let you go. This project is too important to the company. Maybe you need to go work for another firm, where the stakes are lower."

"No," I gasped. "I love working here."

"If you want to stay employed here, if you want me to help you, I must insist on total obedience. No hesitation." She squeezed my chin almost painfully. "Do you understand me?"

"Yes ma'am."

"Very well. Take off your clothes then."

Today I was wearing jeans and a cartoon tee shirt. After kicking off my keds, I pulled my shirt off, revealing a plain cotton bra. Dropping my jeans, I folded them and placed them on a chair with my shirt, standing there in just my bra and panties. When Colleen raised her eyebrow, I removed those as well, face flushing red with humiliation.

I'd never been naked in front of anyone before, other than my doctor, and I felt shy and embarrassed. I crossed one arm over my generous breasts, then covered my unshaved mound with a hand and sucked in my soft belly. I wasn't fat, but I certainly wasn't thin. I was all soft curves. My job left very little time for things like working out.

Colleen walked to her desk, where she disconnected her desk phone from the wall. Returning with the cord she said, "Put your arms behind your back please."

When I hesitated, she barked, "Now!"

My hands flew behind my back before my brain even caught up. Colleen wrapped the cord around each wrist, then drew them together and wrapped the cord around some more until my hands were cinched at the back of my waist.

"Is that pulling your shoulders?" she asked softly.

I tested my bounds. My hands were tied together tight, but my shoulders felt okay.

"No ma'am."

"Great. Now it's time to get you out of your head, young lady. Lay over the conference table please."

CHAPTER THREE: THE SPANKING TABLE

I walked slowly over to the table, wondering if Colleen could see my fleshy ass jiggling. God I hoped not. I really should start doing some squats or something. When I got to the edge of the table, my boss pushed gently between my shoulder blades. I lowered myself until my upper body was resting on the table, my arms still behind my back and my ass on full display.

"I find that a good hard spanking is a great way for people to get out of their head and calm their anxious thoughts," Colleen said almost clinically, as if she was talking about code instead of standing behind my naked ass on display on her conference table.

I opened my mouth to respond, but before I got any words out I felt a sharp sting as Colleen's open palm landed on my ass cheek.

Thwack!

Holy crap, she was really going to spank me! I didn't totally believe it until just now.

Thwack!

Her hand made contact with the other butt cheek. It was almost a pleasant sensation – a compression of flesh followed by a gentle sting. Colleen began a steady rhythm, moving from top to bottom, cheek to cheek, at a steady pace.

Thwack!

Thwack!

Thwack!

It was almost meditative, and while I liked it – more than I imagined I would in fact -- my mind was still racing with thoughts.

Did my ass look bad like this? Were my boobs leaving a mark on the table? Had I fed the cat this morning? How would I fix that bad code?

Thwack!

Thwack!

As the skin on my ass heated, so did my core. I was conscious of a feeling of arousal overtaking my body. My mind wandered, wondering what it would be like if Colleen were to kiss me. Maybe do more.

Thwack!

Thwack!

I heard a loud moan fill the room, and realized it was me. My face flamed in mortification. What kind of weirdo was I, getting off on this?

Colleen's hand stopped moving, resting on my ass for a moment. I felt her fingers slide down slowly, moving just inside the crack of my ass, until she reached my pussy. That greedy girl was clenching on air.

"You're dripping wet!"

Colleen's voice was stern, but I sensed a thread of amusement in her words. "Are you getting off on this? Do you like being punished?"

"Maybe?" My voice was soft.

"Have you been spanked by your lovers? Is that it? Do you associate spanking with sexual desire?"

"I, um, I don't know. I haven't had any lovers," I whispered.

"Ever?"

"No."

"Are you telling me that you're a virgin? At your age?" she sounded fascinated.

"Yes ma'am."

I gasped as I felt one long finger slide deeper in between my lower lips. It moved back and forth through my channel, spreading my moisture, and without a conscious thought I tilted my hips, trying to get her to touch me where I needed to be touched. Maybe it was slutty of me, but I was desperate for Colleen to make me come.

My hopes were dashed at her next words.

"I guess I'll need to get the paddle. I was going too easy on you if you're getting so turned on. You obviously need something more."

She strode across the room, rummaging in her desk, until she returned with a black leather paddle. It was wider at one end, tapering to a handle. My eyes widened as she slapped it against her palm a few times.

"This is going to smart, Marci, but I think you'll find it helpful in teaching you to focus."

She moved back around the table. I heard the sound of air moving a second before the leather cracked onto the already sensitive skin of my ass.

Thwack!

Red hot pain filled my body, and I yelped in surprise, uncaring that someone might hear me. When I struggled to move to an upright position, a firm hand covered my bound hands at my lower back, trapping me in place.

"Be still and take your punishment."

Thwack!

"Fuck! That hurts!" I whined.

Thwack!

I tried to move away, to escape the stinging pain, but Colleen held me in place.

Thwack!

"You've been a bad employee, living in your head and messing up important work."

Colleen's voice was firm and cold.

"You will take your punishment like a good girl."

Thwack!

The pain was becoming more intense, and I struggled against her hold.

Thwack!

"Or you will be fired."

Thwack!

My ass felt like it was on fire. With every smack of the paddle heat spread from the point of contact, like my skin was on fire. Even the muscles in my ass felt sore from the abuse.

Thwack!

"Please. I can't take it. Stop."

The paddle stopped its descent.

"Are you resigning your position here?"

"No."

"Then you know what the rules are."

Thwack!

Thwack!

Thwack!

Colleen gave me three hard spanks in rapid succession.

"I was very clear that if you want to stay here and work at WLW Technology, we must break you of this ridiculous anxiety problem."

Thwack!

"We can only keep employees on who work at one hundred percent. We only want the best of the best here!"

Thwack!

"Owwww!"

I wailed so loud I was sure everyone on the floor could hear me.

Thwack!

"If you don't stop whining, I'm going to get the wooden paddle next," she warned.

I stilled immediately. I'd never been spanked before, not with leather or wood, but I could tell from her voice that the wooden paddle would be worse – although it was hard to imagine right now.

Thwack!

Thwack!

Colleen rained down a steady stream of smacks, and when my ass was completely throbbing in pain, she gave me a few strikes at the very top of my thighs, right where my ass connected to my legs.

Those had the added impact of sending a strong vibration right to my pussy.

Thwack!

Thwack!

I was sobbing now, tears and snot falling down my face, a total mess. All of my attention was focused on the intense pain coming from my ass.

Thwack!

Thwack!

And then it hit me: for the first time in my entire life, my mind was silent.

CHAPTER FOUR: AFTERCARE AND JEALOUSY

I felt my wrists release from their bindings, making me aware that the spanking had finally stopped. I felt like I was floating out of my body, no longer tethered to the Earth, my brain blissfully silent.

The next thing I knew I was laying on the couch, bundled up in a blanket. Colleen sat beside me with a bottle of water in her hand. Gently she lifted my head and tipped a few swallows of water into my mouth.

"I've never seen anyone drop into subspace so hard so fast."

I couldn't decide whether Colleen sounded surprised or impressed.

"Subspace?" I pushed myself up to seated, careful to keep the blanket around me since I was still completely naked.

"It's kind of like a state of bliss, where you just float outside your body, as it's been described to me."

"Oh yeah, that's totally how it was."

I drank more water, my brain turning back on, but much less busy than before, I noticed.

"I feel way less anxious," I said, surprise clear in my tone. "I mean, I always have at least a low level and there's nothing right now. Just regular thoughts, nothing frantic."

"Great," Colleen said, standing up. "Get dressed and fix that code then. And tell me when the anxiety comes back, it usually takes several sessions to get it under control."

I felt a sense of sadness as I found my clothes. I thought maybe Colleen and I would do more, like my friends had, but it was clear she only wanted to spank me to help me get to work, not as a prelude to anything else. She obviously wasn't as attracted to me as I was to her, and I needed to just accept that.

The next week passed quickly. The first day after Colleen spanked me I went to her when I started feeling anxious, and once again she restrained me and spanked me until I calmed down. Not enough to send me to subspace again, just enough to focus my mind.

We repeated the pattern for several days in a row, and each time the benefits of the spanking lasted longer, and my mind stopped spiraling with less correction.

But I wanted more.

Being in such an intimate position with Colleen every night was ratcheting up my attraction for her, and unless I was mistaken, she was feeling the same. I'd caught her staring at me a few times, and she kept giving me little touches that were making me crazy. A stroke of her palm to soothe my aggrieved ass cheeks. Her fingers tangling in my hair before she bound my hands.

On the fifth day after she'd spanked me for the first time I decided to test my theory.

I came into work wearing a short skirt instead of my usual jeans, leaving my long legs bare. I paired it with a tight blouse just this side of decent, and shoes with a heel, then curled my long blonde hair into soft waves. I'd even put on some bright red lipstick. I looked sexy, which was not a usual look for me, and everyone at work noticed.

"Hey Marci, you got a hot date tonight?" Brandy asked when she saw me.

I shook my head and smiled. My friend moved closer to whisper in my ear.

"Trying to get Colleen's attention then?" she whispered.

"Maybe."

I'd confided in my friends about my anxiety treatment – and they all suspected that I had feelings for my boss, even though I hadn't admitted anything.

"I think you got it."

I followed her gaze to where Colleen was striding down the hallway, her green eyes angry and hard.

"Marci, a word please."

I followed my boss into her office. She closed the door behind us with a firm click.

"Why are you dressed like that?" she asked.

"Dressed like what?" I said, striving for an innocent tone.

"You usually dress like a teenager on laundry day," she said. "But today, you're wearing a short skirt and a skintight blouse like some kind of slut."

"This outfit isn't any more risqué than what anyone else wears," I protested. "Jane was wearing a micromini and 'fuck me pumps' today."

"You're trying to get Jane's attention?" she asked, her voice dark and almost dangerous.

"No," I said hotly. "I'm trying to get yours, damn it!"

Her eyes widened and she looked nonplussed for the first time since I'd known her.

"I can't stop thinking about you," I added softly.

"On your knees," she ordered. "I want you to lick my pussy."

I dropped to my knees without a second of hesitation. When Colleen didn't move, I walked on my knees until I was right in front of her, then slowly slid the skirt of her dress up to her waist.

"Take off my panties," she said softly. I immediately complied, pulling the green silk down to her ankles. She stepped out of them, kicking the fabric behind her.

I stared at the sight in front of me. The freckled skin of her lower abdomen, the shock of red hair at her apex, the glistening pink lips beneath. I moved forward but paused as I felt a sharp flick of fingers against my forehead.

"Did I tell you to move?"

"No ma'am."

A few seconds passed before she said, "Make me come now."

I brought my head closer, then licked her from bottom to top. I'd never been this up close and personal with anyone before. Wrapping my hand around her thighs for balance, I slid my tongue inside her folds and lapped up Colleen's cream like it was my job.

Her fingers burrowed into my hair, holding on close to my scalp, and when she tightened her fingers, I felt a bite of pain that made me gasp.

"Keep licking."

I dutifully complied. Colleen used her hand in my hair to direct me where she wanted me to go. After several long minutes she focused my attention right at her apex.

"Flick my clit with your tongue. Hard and fast."

She made a little gasping noise as the top of my tongue made contact with her clitoris. I flicked and tapped, then circled around a few times, adding pressure.

"Good girl, now suck my clit."

Gingerly I wrapped my lips around her swollen bundle of nerves, sucking it between them and adding a bit of suction. Colleen's legs shook before she locked her knees.

"Harder," she ordered.

I glanced up to see my boss had unbuttoned the top of her dress. The fingers of her free hand were pinching her nipple through the silk of her bra while her hips ground against my mouth.

Suddenly she stiffened, then gasped loudly. Her body spasmed a bit as her orgasm hit her, and I resumed moving my tongue up and down her core, swirling roughly around her clit with every pass.

The entire time I kept my eyes fixed on her face. She looked beautiful, her face screwed up in ecstasy as she came with a whoosh of moisture that flooded my tongue. I drank up every drop.

When she was done Colleen released my head and stepped back, breathing heavily. I stayed where I was, waiting for further instructions.

"Are you really a virgin?" she finally asked.

"Yes ma'am."

"Well you won't be, not for long."

CHAPTER FIVE: POPPING MY CHERRY

"Take off your clothes and lay on the table."

Out of habit, I lay face down, expecting a spanking. I heard Colleen let out what almost sounded like a giggle.

"Yeah, okay, this works too. I know it gets you hot."

Before I could interpret her words, her palm came down onto my ass in a sharp smack. After several days of spanking in a row, the skin was hypersensitive, and I yelped at the contact.

Thwack!

"You like being spanked, don't you, you little pain slut?"

Thwack!

Thwack!

"Answer me."

Thwack!

"Yes ma'am, I like it."

God help me, but I'd be perfectly happy to be spanked every day, at least a little. It calmed me in a way no antianxiety med ever had.

Thwack!

Thwack!

"Maybe someday I'll take you to the club and handcuff you to the St. Andrew's Cross for a good whipping."

Thwack!

"Would you like that?"

Thwack!

"Yes ma'am."

Just the thought of it had my pussy gushing.

Colleen's fingers slid between my legs, finding the wetness there. I'd long since stopped feeling embarrassed about it.

"Yeah, you sure do like that idea."

She sounded pleased.

Thwack!

Thwack!

Thwack!

After a few minutes of steady spanking, she stopped again.

"Now that your ass is nice and pink, turn over for me."

This was new. I flashed back to her earlier question about my virginity. Was she going to...?

I rolled over on the table, wincing as the delicate skin of my butt pressed against the table. Colleen lifted one leg, drawing it over her shoulder, and then the other one. In this position I was spread wide for her gaze, and when I looked up, she was staring at my pussy like it was the best thing she'd ever seen.

"I'm glad you don't wax," she told me. "I like my women to look like women, not little girls."

I flushed with pleasure at the term 'my women' and wondered if she meant it. I hoped she did.

Leaning forward, she gave my pussy a long lick. My hips lifted off the table and I made a choking noise. Firm hands clamped down on my hips as she began eating me out in earnest. It felt incredible, even better than I'd imagined it would.

I rolled my hips as much as I could, silently begging her to give my clit some attention. I heard her chuckle against my folds just before she scooted forward a little bit more and bit down on my clit – hard.

I yelped out in a combination of pain and pleasure. Colleen licked around it, soothing me. When she stepped back, I couldn't help but whine. She gave my pussy a hard slap, which almost made me come on the spot.

"Be patient, greedy little girl."

Her fingers traced my folds, then she shoved one finger inside my channel. I gasped at the feeling of something besides my own hand filling me. I'd never had the nerve to insert a vibrator in there, instead focusing the toys on my clit while I pleasured myself with a finger.

Having someone else touch me there felt...good. Different.

Colleen pushed a second finger inside me, stretching me wider, and pumped in and out of me roughly, her thumb pressed against the button at my apex. The room was filled with the obscene sounds of my arousal against her fingers.

She pressed one hand against my lower belly, pinning me to the table, then slid in a third finger. She spread them apart deep inside me and I cried out in pain as my pussy stretched wider than it ever had. The pain immediately turned to intense pleasure as those talented fingers pumped in and out at a steady pace, working me hard. Meanwhile her thumb continued to tease my clit.

When Colleen lowered herself to take one of my nipples into her mouth, trapping me between her and the table, my orgasm hit me hard. My toes curled as electricity ran down my spine and filled my body with the most incredible feeling I'd ever experienced. I shook with the force of my pleasure.

"Colleen!"

My pussy clenched around her fingers as they stroked something deep inside me that kept my orgasm going and going...much longer and more intense than anything I'd ever done alone.

Colleen kept stroking me while she switched her mouth from one nipple to the other. It was so intense that I cried out.

"It's too much."

"It's not," she said firmly. "Take it."

She bit my other nipple even harder than the first, triggering a second orgasm that seemed to go on forever. Totally at her mercy, trapped under Colleen's weight, I had no choice but to give myself over to the feelings of pleasure and take everything she was offering me.

After I came for the third time she finally slowed her movements, lifting herself off me and removing her fingers from my channel. My pussy suddenly felt incredibly empty.

Colleen stepped back, then grabbed my hand, pulling up until I was seated on the conference table where I'd spent so much time this past week. She pressed a soft kiss to my lips, and I realized that even after all we'd done, we hadn't actually kissed.

My eyes met hers, the green hue darker now with her passion, and I deepened the kiss. Colleen's hand came to my head, holding me still, and she took over, shoving her tongue into my mouth and kissing me hard until we were both breathless. When she pulled away, I felt almost disoriented from the adrenaline dump and all the emotions coursing through me.

We stared at each other for at least a full minute before Colleen broke the silence.

"How was it?"

"Better than I'd ever dreamed," I answered honestly.

She looked pleased.

"You know," her voice took on a forced casualness that hinted at deeper emotion, "I've been looking for a new submissive. Someone I can play with long term. Someone who likes pain and isn't afraid to push their limits. Someone like you."

"Someone like me?" I asked, feeling bold. "Or me specifically?"

Her lips quirked. "Well, I admit that I requested you for my team because I've had my eye on you for a while. So what do you say? Should we give this a try?"

I nodded. "Yes ma'am."

"In that case put your clothes on. We're going home."

***

If you liked this book, please leave me a rating or review.

Be sure to sign up for Josie's mailing list at https://www. amazon.com/author/josiebale to be the first to hear about new releases.

SPECIAL PREVIEW: THE RELUCTANT BRIDE'S FIRST SPANKING BY JOSIE BALE

A SPANKING THERAPY CLINIC ADVENTURE

"**A**re we ever going to get married Rebecca?"

Jacob's forceful words burst out suddenly in the silent room, fast and loud, making me jump. I looked up from my e-reader with a frown.

"What?" I asked. "Where is this coming from?"

Jacob moved closer to me on the couch, reaching to take my hand. His touch was familiar and comforting. He stared at me intently until I looked up and met his deep blue eyes.

"I don't understand what the problem is, Rebecca," he said earnestly. "I asked you to marry me two years ago, and you keep refusing to set a date. We've been together five years now. Don't you love me anymore?"

I suppressed a sigh. "Yes, of course I do Jacob, it's, just –"

"What?" he asked impatiently, shaking his head. A lock of his thick blonde hair fell over his forehead with the motion, giving him a boyish appearance that belied his 35 years.

I studied him for a long moment, choosing my words carefully. "I don't feel ready yet," I finally answered lamely. "I need more time."

Jacob's handsome face pinched with frustration. "More time? It's been five years!" he pointed out. "What's holding you back? We have a good thing, right? We love each other. We're compatible. I just don't get it."

I shook my head miserably and looked at my fingers twisting in my lap. "I'm sorry Jacob," I whispered. "I do love you, you know I do, but I'm just not ready. Not yet."

"When will you be ready Rebecca?" he asked. "Will you ever be ready? Or am I supposed to wait forever?"

I shook my head, my eyes filling with tears. When I didn't say anything more, he got up off the couch and stalked out of the room without another word, leaving me alone with my thoughts.

I couldn't blame him for being angry, I had been putting him off for a long time. The truth was, I had a nagging sense of dissatisfaction with our relationship. I truly loved Jacob, but something was missing. I couldn't quite put my finger on it, so I had no idea how to discuss it with him.

My girlfriends all told me I was crazy to not have locked him down already. Jacob was the perfect man: attentive, generous, supportive, and kind. He had a good job, worked out, ate healthy, didn't drink excessively or smoke or do drugs. He treated me like a princess.

And not that this was a deal breaker or anything, but he was quite good looking: about six feet tall with wide shoulders, washboard abs, brilliant blue eyes, and a strong chin with a dimple in the center. Honestly, he could have been a model.

We had a lot of fun together and we were quite compatible.
The only negative really was that our love making was....
just fine. Vanilla. Kind of bland. It was nothing to write
home about. Jacob was a missionary man, if you know
what I mean. He mostly gravitated to that one position,
resisting my efforts to try something else. And we rarely
had sex outside of the bed. Shower sex was a special treat
in our world.

Don't get me wrong, Jacob almost always got me off, he
was really considerate that way. He was a master of eating
pussy, quite talented in that department. But I longed
for some passion, some excitement, something less pre-
dictable.

Sometimes when I was home alone, I would burrow under
the covers with my vibrator and fantasize about a different
kind of lover: someone who would push me up against a
wall, shove aside my panties and really fuck me, hard and
rough, like he couldn't wait another moment to be inside
me. Someone who would take me from behind while
slapping my ass. Someone who would talk dirty and pinch
my nipples.

It was ridiculous really. Here I was, a dyed-in-the-wool
feminist engaged to an enlightened man who treated me

like an equal and I longed for someone more alpha. Just in the bedroom, mind you. I did not want to be bossed around in real life, but a little domination in the bedroom? That's what got me off in my private moments. But there was no way I could tell Jacob that.

Later that night I lay awake in the bed, listening to Jacob snoring softly, and tried to convince myself to set a date for the wedding. I told myself I should either marry him or break up with him. But I couldn't do either. Was this all there was?

The next day I woke up in a funk. I had a bad feeling that Jacob was nearing the end of his patience and even though I wasn't ready to marry him, I didn't want to lose him either. I sat in the coffee shop near my office, brooding as I sipped my chai latte and thumbed through our city's alternative weekly. Suddenly an ad seemed to jump off the page.

"Do you need to be punished? Do you have emotional blocks preventing you from living your best life? Our experienced Spanking Therapists can help set you straight. Call today."

My heart was pounding as I read and re-read that ad. Did I dare? I had never even heard of spanking therapy, but

I couldn't deny that the thought of being spanked by a stranger was strangely titillating. And I couldn't get past the thought that this might be exactly what I needed to get past whatever was bothering me and help me to make up my mind about my relationship with Jacob. Maybe if I just tried it once I could get it out of my system and settle down with Jacob.

Before I could change my mind, I locked myself into the single stall restroom and made the call. A professional sounding woman picked up and explained how the process worked.

"I'll send you a questionnaire via email to fill out and return to us. You might find it a bit intrusive but it's really necessary for us to design the best therapeutic experience for you so please answer honestly," the woman explained. "Once we receive the questionnaire and your deposit, I will contact you to schedule your first appointment."

"How many appointments does it usually take?" I asked timidly, feeling a little over my head.

"It depends on the person," the lady answered. "Some people come once and experience a level of catharsis that lets them move on. Others prefer to come in regularly, kind of like maintenance. It'll be up to you and the therapist to figure out a treatment plan that works best for you and your particular issues."

Before I could change my mind, I went back to my table in the coffee shop and filled out the extensive questionnaire in my e-mail, sending it back with a $250 deposit. My hands shook as I pressed "send". Excitement and dread warred for my attention. Would I have the guts to actually do this? Would it help?

Within an hour I received an email back offering me an appointment for the following day. Suddenly I felt resolved to check it out. Spanking therapy....it was worth a try, right?

For more of the story, check out "The Reluctant Bride's First Spanking" by Josie Bale, part of the "Spanking Therapy Series" available now at https://www.amazon.com/dp/B0CY3YRQ4V

OTHER BOOKS BY JOSIE BALE

*F*ollow Josie Bale to receive email updates for all new releases. For more information visit https://mailchi.mp/5031b4165265/josie-newsletter-sign-up

The Sapphic Submission Series

Punished By the Boss

Pleasing the Boss

Tied Up By the Boss

Dominated By the Boss

The Divorce Recovery Series

Spanking Justice: A Middle-Aged Divorcee's First Spanking

A Punishing Workout: Spanked by the Trainer

A Disciplined Budget: Spanked by the Accountant

The Spanking Therapy Series

The Reluctant Bride's First Spanking

The Reluctant Bride Gets Caught

The Billionaire Gets Punished

The Curvy Reporter Gets Punished

Unlikely Doms Series

Alpha in a Sweater Vest

Alpha Plumber

Hotel Spanking

Alpha Student

Alpha Yogi

The Punishing Holidays Series

Turkey and a Spanking

Shopping and a Spanking

Presents and a Spanking

Be sure to follow Josie's author page on your favorite retailer!

ABOUT JOSIE BALE

J osie Bale loves nothing more than to feel the sting of a palm on her backside. Or a brush. Or a strap. She's not picky, as long as she's getting what she wants.

Her stories feature the lighter side of BDSM including spanking, bondage, and power play. Be sure to follow Josie on your favorite retailer and sign up for her newsletter to be the first to hear about new releases, giveaways, and special sales. For more information visit https://mailchi .mp/5031b4165265/josie-newsletter-sign-up.

Printed in Great Britain
by Amazon

60312260R00037